# SAVE THE GOLD TOP

Mark Hickey

ISBN: 9798346032823



## Disclaimer

This is a work of fiction. Names, characters, places and incidents either are the product of the author's imagination or are used fictitiously and any resemblance to actual persons, living or dead, business establishments, events or locales is entirely coincidental.

## Dedication

In memory of Jacob and Marley, the 1st two cats I owned.

## Acknowledgements

My thanks go to my Dad for his help with solving some of the writing problems and my wife, Heather, for her patience and support, and finally, I would like to thank my fellow truck driver Martin Fallon following countless hours of discussion on all things cats, military and humorous anecdotes. It paid off.

# Table of Contents

# CHAPTER 1

06.55 and sunlight shone through the windows. Cats scurried around the palace as shouts of five minutes to go echoed along the corridors.

Jacob's personal chef, his tabby fur glistening with sweat, stepping out of the kitchen, stopped in the corridor and shouted, 'Are we under attack?'

A ginger tom, rushing by, glared at the chef, 'No. We are getting to our stations ready for Master Lord Jacob's morning inspection.'

The main cat palace stood in the centre of sector C, on the planet Paradise, since it had been rebuilt ten years ago.

Oliver, the senior cat dressed in a light green suit that covered most of his black fur, strolled along the corridor. Overhearing the conversation, he stopped, 'You get to your station.' And pointing at the chef. 'You get back in the kitchen and get Master's breakfast ready.'

He continued marching to the wooden stairs, climbing them two at a time. Reaching the top, he past six bedrooms and stood to attention outside of the door facing him. The palace clock struck seven.

The door opened, in the doorway stood a cat wearing a black suit covering most of his dark blonde fur, 'Good morning.'

Oliver bowed. 'Good morning, Master Lord Jacob.'

Jacob took two steps forward and stood next to his senior cat. 'Has my Gold Top milk order arrived as I'm running low?'

'Only half of the order has been delivered Master.'

Jacob folded his arms. 'Find out where the rest of my order is. Now for the morning inspection and I do hope chef has done my breakfast correctly.'

'So do I.'

Jacob and Oliver proceeded with the inspection. Jacob found two faults: the door cat was not wearing a tie, for which he was immediately fired. The other fault was the plain, red, round rug in the drawing room was apparently the wrong way round.

With the inspection complete, Jacob and Oliver headed to the main dining room for breakfast. Entering the dining room Jacob headed straight to the fridge cabinet and removed the Gold Top milk. He poured two glasses, pulled up a chair and sat down at the solid oak table opposite Oliver. A few minutes later, the chef appeared and placed two plates on the table.

Jacob stared at his plate. 'Chicken, salmon, baked beans. No bacon.' He folded his arms and stared straight at the chef. 'What is this?'

'It's a full Taber breakfast Lord Jacob.'

Jacob unfolded his arms and banged his paws on the table. 'You call that a full Taber?'

The chef took a deep breath, his heart beating faster and beads of sweat forming on his brow. 'Yes.'

'My name when you address me is Master Lord Jacob and why is there no bacon?' Jacob picked the plate up and threw it straight at the chef. 'You're fired.'

As the chef scurried from the room Jacob banged his paws on the table. 'Someone get my breakfast and a new chef now. Before I lose my temper and fire someone else.'

Oliver rushed after the chef, caught up with him as he opened the kitchen service door to exit the palace. 'Wait.' Picking up a pen and a piece of paper from the kitchen worktop, he scribbled down an address and handed it to the chef. 'Go to the school, tell them I sent you and you will get a job. Goodbye.'

Closing the service door, Oliver went to his office. Entering, he marched over to his desk and took a pen from the draw. Removing the calendar from the wall, he crossed out the number 874 and replaced it with 875. Walking over to the window and looking out at the palace gardens, he stood motionless for a second. *If only Marley were here, he would keep Jacob under control.* Replacing the calendar, he ran to the kitchen, hoping someone was getting Jacob his breakfast. Approaching the kitchen, the aroma of bacon cooking reached his nostril's.

Reaching the kitchen door, Oliver stood motionless, gawping at Jacob wearing a chef's hat and frying bacon. 'I didn't know you were applying for Cat Chef.' he said as he ambled towards Jacob.

'Think your funny. Just because you started as a chef in the army. I can cook bacon you know.' Jacob placed four more rashes of bacon into the frying pan.

'In that case, I'll have a bacon sandwich with brown sauce. If it's any good, I'll recommend you for the position of chef.'

'No thanks my chefs tend to get fired. Think you better find me a new one.'

'That's a good idea. I would hate to fire you.' Oliver tapped Jacob on the shoulder, grinned, departed from the kitchen and made his way back to his office ready to begin the search for Jacob's personal chef number 876.

After Jacob had finished his bacon sandwiches, he left the kitchen and strolled to Oliver's office.

The door swung open and Jacob stepped in. 'I am going out to inspect the new technology dome.'

'I'll call the driver.' Oliver reached for the telephone.

'I will drive myself as I want to surprise them.'

'That's not very sporting of you, they might not like the surprise.'

'Oh well. Tough.' Jacob tapped the desk with his paw. 'They need to know who is boss and just maybe I will go easy on them.'

'That'll be a first.'

'Cheeky.'

Jacob left the office and closed the door behind him. Making his way to the garage, he checked the cats were carrying out their duties. The door into the garage swung open and Jacob stepped inside. In the garage, at his disposal, were a troop carrier, two buggies, three all-terrain defenders and a sports F-4 mini. Walking over to the key box, he took the keys for the sports F-4 mini and pressed the button to open the garage door. Climbing into the car, and with the garage door open, he drove off rapidly. Driving along the roads. *How things have changed since I arrived here ten years ago on Paradise.*

When he arrived on Paradise ten years ago, he was given the job of regenerating sector C. The estate that he created spread over an area of twenty-six square miles and was nearly self-sufficient. There were 45 domes in total, split into 8 shopping, 15 for the growing of crops, 7 for livestock, 6 for housing and schools and the remaining 9 were split for entertainment, leisure and one derelict technology dome. The only dome they did not have was a dairy dome as they had to import the milk from Milk Island.

The dome Jacob was on his way to inspect today was the new technology dome that was being constructed for top secret designs and concept technology. Driving along the road, admiring his achievement of regenerating sector C, which included more trees, grass and a network of roads and rail, he noticed that domes seven and twelve were looking rather untidy with the grass needing cutting. *I will have the managers' report to me for a chat.*

As he drove up the road towards the new technology dome, he observed that the dome had been completed on the outside. Parking in the corner of the car park so as not to alert the workers to his arrival on site, he climbed out the car and eyed up the new dome. Steel glistened in the sunlight and new solar glass panels covered the entire top half of the dome. Jacob ambled towards the entrance, scrutinizing the finish. Reaching the entrance, he pushed the door open and stepped inside, observing most of the workers were busy getting on with their jobs. Standing in the entrance, he noticed that the tiled floor was uneven and a small group of workers were just standing talking.

He marched straight over to the group of workers. 'Who's in charge?'

This took them by surprise, one of the workers pointed to a tortoise shell. 'He is the supervisor Master Lord Jacob.'

This caused the workers in the immediate area to stop working.

The cat in question dashed towards Jacob. 'What a pleasant surprise it is to see you, Master Lord Jacob.'

'You can cut the pleasantries. I see you are behind on your schedule. The dome was to have been fully completed by now.' Jacob stood with his arms folded staring at the cat.

'But you keep altering the plans.'

Jacob unfolded both arms and clenched his paws. 'You're fired.'

The supervisor who had just been fired scurried out of the dome entrance. Jacob looked around at the workmen pointing at one of them, 'You.'

The cat stuttered, 'Yes, Master Lord Jacob.'

'You are now the supervisor and I want this dome completed on time and to my specifications. Do you understand?' Jacob folded his arms.

The cat took a deep breath before speaking. 'Yes, I do Master Lord Jacob.'

'Good, come with me and I will explain what I want.'

As they both set off on the tour of the dome, one of the workers put his paw over his mouth. 'Well, that is now 799 supervisors he has fired in the last year.'

Jacob and his newly appointed supervisor were walking at a leisurely pace as everything had to be meticulously inspected by them. The layout and the materials that were being used were on his radar. The first problem brought to the newly appointed supervisor's attention was the tiled floor in the entrance lobby was uneven, and it was to be rectified immediately. Leaving the lobby, the next port of call was the kitchen. Jacob opened the kitchen door and stepped inside.

Looking around the kitchen, he could see that modern-day appliances had been installed: a frost-free fridge, microwave, a dishwasher, etc, when he noticed the table. 'Why is this table not marble?'

The new supervisor began desperately flicking through sheets of paper on his clipboard, searching for an answer. A minute had passed when he found what he was looking for. 'It is made from solid oak.'

Jacob slammed an open cupboard door shut then banged his paws off the worktop. 'I can see it's made from oak. I'm not blind. Who authorized it?'

Swallowing first. 'You did Master Lord Jacob.'

Jacob snatched the clipboard from the new supervisor's paw. Looking through the sheets of paper to see who had authorised the change. After a few seconds of flicking through the paper on the clipboard, he found what he was looking for.

He handed the clipboard back. 'It's OK, Professor Marley made the change.'

The tour of the dome continued with Jacob making notes as they went round.

They arrived at the location of the loading bay, 'Why has construction not been started on the loading bay?'

'We are waiting for the delivery of the steel which is scheduled for tomorrow morning, Master Lord Jacob.'

'Very good.' Jacob handed over a small list of faults that he wanted correcting before completion.

The list that the new supervisor received was only twenty-two pages of A4 paper. 'I will make a start on the list straight away.'

Jacob just folded his arms. 'You better had.'

The new supervisor dashed away to begin sorting the list of problems.

Jacob ambled back the entrance of the dome. Once outside, he strolled back to his car. Nearing his car, he caught the smell of a beautiful aroma in the air. Making his way over to some workers who were outside having a break, as they were sat on wooden boxes, eating and drinking. Approaching the workers, he noticed that one of them was cooking.

'What are you cooking? It smells and looks delicious.' Jacob leaned over to get a better look at what was cooking.

The worker raised her head. 'I'm cooking lasagne, Master Lord Jacob. Would you care to sample?'

'Yes, I would thank you. What is your name?'

'I'm Meg.' She handed Jacob a spoon.

Helping himself and after eating a spoonful of lasagne, he licked his lips. 'That was delicious Meg. I have found my perfect chef. You are hired.'

'I'm not a chef.' Meg picked up a bag of tools and showed them to Jacob.

'You are now. I need a new personal chef at the palace. So come with me.'

'Yes, Master Lord Jacob, thank you.'

They both strolled over to the car and climbed in. Jacob started the car and drove off towards the palace, feeling rather pleased with himself as he had found himself a chef.

# CHAPTER 2

Sunlight shone through the bedroom window. Marley put his white lab coat on covering most of his light blonde fur. Leaving the bedroom, he strolled towards the kitchen, entered, walked over to the worktop and prepared himself a breakfast of cheese on toast with brown sauce. He took the milk from the fridge and poured a glass. With the milk returned to the fridge, he placed the plate of cheese on toast and the glass of milk on a tray and walked steadily to his desk in the workroom. Marley placed the tray on his desk, being careful not to disturb any of his paper work. Sitting down in his green, leather, computer chair he booted up the computer. With the password entered his day had started at 06.00.

Sitting in his chair, Marley consumed his breakfast and drank his milk. With breakfast finished, his attention turned to the day's work, the top-secret project or the concept project. He took a small, silver coin from his desk draw and flipped it. The coin landed tails up. He decided this ruled out the top-secret project which meant he could polish up the concept project, his favourite one anyway.

Marley glanced up at the clock on the wall. *Where was Herbie? 06.15 he was never late for work.*

The door to the workroom swung open. 'Sorry Professor Marley for being late but I have heard on the radio that a small force has surrounded the dairy on Milk Island. This could cause a shortage of milk.'

Marley swung round in his chair. 'Morning Herbie. Don't worry about the small force on milk island, I am sure General Sooty and his army will take care of it.'

'I'm sure you are right professor. I have finished the technology project you assigned me. Do you want to check it?'

'We will have a glass of cold milk first and put your lab coat on. Then, I will have a look at what you have done.' Marley gave a small smile.

Herbie put on his white, lab coat covering his black and white fur.

They left the workroom and strolled to the kitchen. Reaching the kitchen, Marley took the milk from the fridge and two glasses from the cupboard. He poured the milk and they both sat down at the four-seat, wooden, drop-leaf table.

Before taking a drink of milk, Marley turned to face Herbie, 'Would you like some breakfast?'

'I would love some of your cheese on toast with brown sauce, Professor.' Herbie licked his lips.

Marley made the breakfast for Herbie. With breakfast eaten, they walked steadily back to the workroom. Sitting at his desk, Marley opened the technology folder on his computer. He could see that Herbie had indeed finished the project using the correct materials.

He was curious to see what Herbie had created. 'Right let's see the finished article.'

Herbie placed a travel mug on Marley's desk, 'The travel mug is designed for you to drink underwater without getting the contents any wetter.'

'Have you tested it?' Marley said as he picked up the travel mug.

'Yes, but it doesn't play a tune.' Herbie scratched his head.

'Don't worry I will have a look and it will be working in no time.' He gave Herbie a reassuring pat on the back.

Marley spent the next two minutes looking at the folder for the fault. 'Found the error.'

Herbie got up from his desk and stood next to the Professor.

Marley pointed to the computer screen. 'The problem is the code. When we were at university, you were good at most things, but not programming.'

With the code changed, the travel mug played a tune. They both came to the same conclusion the tune of 'The Wheels on The Bus Go Round and Round' needed altering later.

'I better cancel the sports car then professor.'

'That would be a wise idea as you will not get rich with this.'

They both laughed, before returning to their work.

Marley sat at his computer and closed the technology folder. He clicked on the concept folder. The folder opened and he clicked on the dimensions subfolder. He studied the data to make sure everything had been completed to his specifications.

Turning his chair round in the direction of Herbie. 'Can you please look at the storage compartments folder and make sure they have been altered as per my instructions.'

'Yes Professor.'

Over the next four hours, between them they checked all the data in the concept folder. Marley was satisfied that everything had been completed as per his instructions.

With everything now updated, Marley shut down his computer. 'It's lunch time.'

'Ok, I'll just close my computer down professor.'

They left the workroom and made their way to the kitchen. When they reached it, Marley headed straight for the fridge.

He opened the fridge door and looked inside. 'Looks like chicken sandwiches for dinner as we have no salmon.'

'Chicken it is then Professor. Pass the milk and I'll pour both of us a glass.' Herbie took two glasses from the cupboard.

Marley took the milk from the fridge and passed it to Herbie. He removed the chicken and prepared the sandwiches.

Herbie returned the milk to the fridge and sat down at the table.

Marley returned the leftover chicken to the fridge. He placed the plates of sandwiches on the table and sat down opposite Herbie. They both ate their sandwiches and drank their milk. They cleaned up after lunch.

Marley hung the tea towel on the rail, 'Right, we will go and see how the concept project has been finished.'

They left the kitchen and sauntered along the corridor towards the concept room, chatting as they went. When they reached the door of the concept room, Marley entered the door code, using the key pad on the wall and entered the room first, the lights were activated as soon as he stepped into the room. Marley walked over to the wooden desk to the left of the door. He removed the drawings for the concept, mini submarine project from the draw and placed them on the desk top.

Rolling the drawings flat, he began to study them. 'Herbie go and get the steps so we can inspect the mini sub.'

'Ok Professor.'

Herbie returned with the steps and placed them next to the mini sub.

Marley looked up from the drawings. 'I will check the interior to make sure everything is to specification and you can check the exterior.'

'Yes Professor.'

Marley left the desk and walked over to the steps. He climbed up ready to inspect the interior. Reaching over to unscrew the hatch on the mini sub he immediately noticed the hatch had been widened as per his instructions.

Just before he disappeared into the sub, he turned and glanced down at Herbie. 'Make sure all of the welds are smooth and flat.'

'Will do Professor.'

Once inside, Marley sat in the front seat first. There was now enough room in which to operate the controls. The viewing window had been made larger, giving the driver a much better view. With the checks completed in the front, he moved to the rear seat. This seat had been moved further back to make room for a small screen. Marley switched the screen on and using the exterior cameras he watched Herbie meticulously check the welds. He switched the screen off and turned his attention to the storage compartment and found it had been completed to his specifications.

Marley exited the mini sub and climbed down the steps to where Herbie was waiting. 'Did you find anything during your inspection?'

'No Professor all the welds are smooth, but the sub seems to be longer than originally stated.'

'Well done for noticing. I had it made six inches longer for the storage compartments. Now, we need to know if it is water tight.'

'Do you want to test the mini sub today Professor?'

'Yes, but you need to name this one.'

'Well, Professor, the other one is called Hide-52. So why not name this one Seek-53.

'Seek-53 it is then.'

Herbie left the room to go and organize for Seek-53 to be placed in the test pool.

Before Marley made his way to the test pool, he rolled up the drawings and placed them back in the draw. Leaving the concept room, he made his way to the workroom to collect a notepad. Arriving at the testing pool, he found the mini sub had been placed in the pool and the test crew were in position awaiting instructions. Marley instructed them to completed one run on top, one run submerged and to check that the cameras operated under water. The test crew carried out the instructions. He waited patiently at the edge of the pool for the test to be completed.

The test crew disembarked from the mini sub and a cat marched over to Marley. 'The test was a complete success Professor. The cameras are operational under water and most importantly, she is water tight.'

'Thank you and well done.' Marley punched the air with his paw.

With the test over and having been a success, Marley and Herbie went to the kitchen to get some tea. Before they left Marley took Herbie for a run round the pool in Seek-53. He enjoyed taking the sub round the pool as he told Herbie it reminded him of his days in C.A.T. (Covert Aquatics Team.).

# CHAPTER 3

Jacob parked his sports F.4 mini in the garage next to the troop carrier. He turned to Meg, 'Wait by the car while I close the garage door'

With the door closed he waved his arm. 'Follow me and I will introduce you to Oliver, my head cat.'

They left the garage and entered the palace. Meg stood in the doorway, gawping, trying to take everything in all at once.

'Come on, you can do the tour later.' He waved his arm to signal for meg to follow him.

As they marched to Oliver's office, Meg tried to take everything in, from the paintings to the plush carpets.

Arriving at Oliver's office door, Jacob knocked, opened the door and stepped inside. 'I have good news. I have found my chef.'

'You have found a new chef?'

'Yes. Come in.'

Meg entered with her head held high. Jacob introduced Meg to Oliver.

'Hello sir.'

Oliver smiled at Meg. 'You don't call me sir, just Oliver.'

Jacob grinned. 'Well as nice as this is, I am very busy so I will leave you with Oliver. I am going to the study.'

With Jacob out of the room, Oliver sat down in his ox-blood red, leather chair and stretched. He looked at Meg. 'Come on, I best show you the kitchen.'

Oliver stood up and they left for the kitchen. When they reached the kitchen, Oliver showed Meg where everything was.

'Well Meg, I will leave you get on with his tea.'

Meg just stood staring at Oliver with her arms out stretched. 'What am I to cook?'

Oliver smiled. 'Oh, I forgot. He fired his chef this morning, just surprise him and good luck.'

Oliver strolled out of the kitchen, leaving Meg to cook tea and made his way to the study.

Oliver knocked, on the study door, opened it and stepped inside. 'Well, someone is getting a surprise for tea. Hope you picked a good chef.'

Jacob shuffled in his ox-blood leather chair and looked up from behind his solid oak desk. 'Well, if I didn't, I guess you will fire me, Sir Oliver.'

'I'm not getting you a calendar and you can drop the sarcasm.'

Oliver closed the door and sat down in the leather chair facing Jacob. Before the meeting started Jacob poured out two glasses of his special, gold top milk. The meeting lasted for half an hour. The main points from the meeting were, find out why the full delivery of gold top milk had not arrived, and Meg was to be given free rein in the kitchen, if her cooking came up to scratch.

Jacob finished his drink and stood up from behind his desk. 'Well let's go and see what is for tea. Oh, and you will be joining me since you are now a sir.' Jacob patted Oliver on the shoulder and smiled.

'Thank you. You're far to kind to me.'

They left the study and made their way to Jacob's private, dining room located next to the kitchen. On entering, they sat down at the old rustic wooden farm table that Jacob had restored, including the four wooden chairs from one of the domes, when he arrived at sector C ten years ago.

Meg appeared from the kitchen. 'Tea will be served in five minutes, Master Lord Jacob.'

'Very good. Oliver is joining me tonight.'

Meg left the dining room and went back to the kitchen. Oliver got up from his seat and went to the fridge cabinet next to the table and took out the milk. Two glasses were poured and the milk returned to the fridge.

Meg entered the dining room and placed a large dish of lasagne on the table. 'Hope you enjoy your meal.' She turned and strolled back to the kitchen.

'I am sure we will. It looks delicious. Thank you.' commented Jacob.

Oliver took a serving spoon and placed a portion of lasagne on Jacob's plate, then served himself. They both ate in silence.

'Well, Oliver that was amazing. Best lasagne I have tasted.' Jacob said, before licking his lips.

'I agree it was delicious.'

'I wonder what is for dessert.'

A couple of minutes later, Meg entered carrying a large bowl of rice pudding, which was placed on the table. Oliver again served the portions up. The rice pudding was a big hit.

'Now that we have finished tea will you go and fetch Meg.'

'Yes.'

Oliver left and returned with Meg.

'That meal was amazing Meg. Well done.'

'Thank you, Master Lord Jacob.'

'From now on you may cook anything you like for tea. The only thing I request is that you cook me a full Taber breakfast every day.'

'I will see that it is adhered to Master Lord Jacob.'

'Thank you Meg, you may go now.'

As Meg left the dining room, she did so with her head held high and a big grin on her face.

Jacob turned to face Oliver, 'Can you arrange for the managers of domes seven and twelve to report to me after breakfast in the morning.'

'I will arrange that and go easy on them.'

'I will go easy on them. I always do.'

Jacob got up from his seat and headed off to bed.

The following morning started just like any other, the staff were all running around panicking getting to their posts. The usual inspection was done, no faults were found and nobody got fired.

Jacob headed for breakfast hoping he would finally get his bacon. Once seated Meg served breakfast.

Jacob looked at his plate then at Meg, 'Finally I have bacon, well done.'

'Thank you, Master Lord Jacob.'

'I will go and start to prepare your tea.' Meg left and went back to the kitchen, a big grin on her face.

Oliver entered the dining room to find Jacob had finished his breakfast. 'The two managers are waiting outside of your office. I told them you were in a good mood.'

'I'm always in a good mood. I got my bacon, so I will go easy on them.'

'You starting to go soft in your old age?'

'No. You get on with your manager duties or I might need to get a calendar.'

As Oliver left the dining room, he commented, 'Who else would put up with you?'

Jacob ambled to his office where the two managers were waiting outside. The meeting lasted less than thirty seconds. They were both fired.

Jacob left the office and marched to the study feeling rather pleased with himself. He opened the study door and entered, walking straight over to the wooden cabinet, he removed a glass and placed it on the coffee table. Taking a bottle of gold top milk from the fridge, he poured a glass and returned the milk to the fridge. Sitting in his chair sipping his drink, he tapped his paw on the chair arm. *Well, at least I didn't lose my temper with the managers.*

Jacob finished his milk, ambled to Oliver's office and left a note on his desk. It was to chase up the order of the missing gold top milk and make sure the accounts were all up to date. Jacob strolled around the palace and the gardens for about an hour making sure the staff knew who was boss.

The rest of the day went along very smoothly. The staff were now a lot happier and most of it was put down to the arrival of Meg, who was cooking Jacob's meals, and this made him happy. As the day ended, Jacob asked Oliver to report to the study for a chat.

Oliver reported to the study and sat opposite Jacob.

'You found out what happened to my milk order? In the morning I'm going to surprise them at the technology dome.'

'No news yet on the milk order. You really should warn them. They won't like the surprise.'

'I may have to fire my milk cat. I love giving the workers surprises.' Jacob looked at Oliver and smiled.

With the chat over, Jacob headed for bed and Oliver went to his office to chase up the gold top milk order.

# CHAPTER 4

Marley and Herbie sat in the kitchen eating their tea as the sunlight faded and darkness descended. They discussed how well the test of Seek 53 had gone.

'Well, Professor, are you pleased with the new interior layout you designed?'

'I am most pleased with the interior now that the storage compartments are bigger and more accessible for the equipment to be stored.'

They continued discussing the test results for a few hours before going to bed.

The following morning, Marley entered the kitchen and the smell of bread been toasted and cheese melting hit is nostrils.

Herbie looked up from the grill. 'Morning Professor.'

'Morning.'

'Breakfast will be a couple of minutes.'

'Thank you. I will pour the milk.'

Marley removed the milk from the fridge and poured out two glasses and returned the milk to the fridge.

Herbie served the cheese on toast with brown sauce and they both sat down at the table and ate breakfast. With breakfast finished they left the kitchen and walked to the workroom.

Entering the workroom, Marley switched the lights on. They both sat at their respective desks and switched the computers on. The computers sprang into life, going through their start up cycle.

'My computer is ready Professor. What are we working on today?'

'We are going to test Seek 53 at sea to see how she handles and to see if my new sonar paint works.'

'That will be fun Professor. Am I coming along?'

'Yes. You can come along and take notes. Can you organize the transport for Seek 53 while I get a driver?'

'Thank you, Professor. I will go and organize that straight away.'

Herbie left the workroom to go and organize the transport for Seek 53.

Marley picked up the phone and dialled the only place capable of supplying a driver.

A cat answered the phone. 'Hello. You are through to One Paw. How may I help you?'

'This is retired, Lieutenant Colonel Marley. I require your top cat for a test run today.'

'Yes, Lieutenant, Colonel Marley, we can arrange that for you.'

'Thank you. Have him report to the beach at 11.00, sharp.'

'We will send our top cat, George. Thank you. Goodbye.'

'Goodbye.'

Marley switched off his computer, picked up his note pad and headed for the car park. Reaching the car park, he glanced around but there was no sign of Herbie. He removed his phone from his pocket and called Herbie. Two minutes after the phone call, Herbie appeared and confirmed that the transport was organized. They both proceeded to climbed into Marley's series two sports defender and drove off for the beach.

They arrived at the beach and found the mini sub already in the water ready for testing. Marley looked at his watch and the time was 11.00. A transport shuttle pulled up, stopping at the edge of the beach. The door opened and out stepped a cat dressed in aquatic dark green coveralls, covering his ginger fur, and dark sunglasses.

As he marched across the white sand towards Marley, he stopped. 'Who parked that loco?'

A cat spoke up, 'I did why?'

He marched straight over to the cat and hit him knocking him to the ground. 'I hate bad parking.' He marched straight over to Marley. 'Captain George reporting for duty sir.'

'Pleased to meet you, Captain. Why did you hit my driver? Out here you call me Professor Marley.'

'He was parked badly Professor Marley.'

'He was parked on the beach Captain. Now let's get on with the testing of the mini sub shall we.'

'Yes, Professor Marley.'

Marley escorted George to the mini sub. He gave a quick explanation of the controls and handed a list of instructions to George.

Instructions

1. Depth not more than 50 Feet
2. Speed not more than 5 Knots
3. Remain undetected for the whole test (1 hour.)

George took the note from Marley and smiled. 'I do hate bad parking Professor.'

George climbed into Seek 53 and closed the hatch to get ready for the test run. Marley gave the order to start the test. George manoeuvred the mini sub out to sea and submerged to a depth of 50 feet.

'Do you want the sonar balls dropping now Professor?'

Yes. Drop five to begin with.'

Herbie gave the order and five sonar balls were dropped into the sea. Once the sonar balls were active, George was told to begin the test. George started by moving the mini sub in an easterly direction at a speed of five knots and a depth of fifty feet. He carried on moving around over the next hour, altering course, depth and speed. During the test a further five sonar balls were dropped into the water. After an hour, Herbie who was monitoring the data from the sonar balls had not detected the mini sub.

With the test over George returned to the beach, hopeful that the test was a success.

Marley strolled over to George. 'Well Captain, early reports indicate that the test was a success.'

'Thank you, Professor, I only want to help.'

Marley asked George a series of questions relating to the handling of the new mini sub. George answered the questions given by Marley. He added that in his opinion the mini sub had performed excellently overall, with the questions finished he headed back to One Paw.

Before George departed Marley chuckled. 'That mini sub is not parked straight Captain.'

'I don't do bad parking Professor and it is parked straight.'

They both laughed and George departed.

Herbie ambled over to Marley. 'He is an odd one Professor.'

'That he is Herbie, but you could not locate him during the test.'

'No Professor. But, he did not follow your orders to the letter.'

'That is why I will use him again.'

The mini sub was loaded back onto the transport loco ready to be taken back to the technology dome. Marley and Herbie left the beach and headed back to the technology dome in the series two sports defender.

With everything back at the dome and stored away, they headed to the kitchen for a cold glass of milk. After they had finished their milk, both went into the workroom and turned on the computers ready to analyse the data from the test run. They sat and analysed the mountains of data from the test, and could not find anything at all that pointed to Seek 53 been detected. The test had been a complete success, Seek 53 had been undetectable in the water.

Herbie swung round in his chair to face Marley. 'Very well done, Professor, your design is a success.'

'I'm pleased that my design is a success and my new sonar paint is a success.'

'Are we now finished with this project Professor?'

'Yes. The project is now completed. I will save all of the data and mark the project as completed.'

Marley saved the data and closed his computer down. Sitting in his chair, he leaned back. *Well, that's it the last project at this technology dome is now completed. Time to move to the new technology dome.*

That night Marley and Herbie sat in the lounge for the last time before the move to the new technology dome. They drank ice cold milk and ate salmon sandwiches while reminiscing about the projects that they had worked on over the years.

Marley rose from the chair. 'Well, it's time for bed as we move to our new dome tomorrow.'

'Goodnight, Professor. I will do breakfast in the morning before we leave.'

'Goodnight, Herbie. I know it's not Saturday, but I would like my favourite breakfast a bacon and egg sandwich.'

'Ok Professor.'

The next morning after they had eaten Marley's favourite breakfast cooked by Herbie, they took one last look around the old technology dome. Both got into Marley's series two sports defender and set off for the new technology dome.

# CHAPTER 5

As Marley drove along the roads towards the new technology dome, himself and Herbie reminisced about the time they had spent in the old technology dome. They both wondered what the new dome would look like now that it had been finished. As they drove up the road towards the dome car park, they could see that it was a hive of activity.

'Look Professor, one of the transport locos has arrived.'

'Yes, I see, hopefully everything is in order.'

'I will check once we are parked up Professor.'

Marley parked his car in a parking bay and they both got out. Herbie marched straight off to make sure that the unloading of the loco was going to plan. Marley ambled towards the entrance of the dome.

As he entered the dome the currant supervisor greeted him. 'Good morning Professor.'

'Good morning.'

'Would you like a tour?'

'Yes, I would like that very much, thank you.'

The new supervisor and Marley set off on a tour of the new technology dome. They ambled around the dome, chatting about how the build had gone, and how hopefully the new technology dome would improve live on Paradise. Marley was very pleased with how the dome had been constructed. He was, also, pleased with how his alterations had been done. After a while, Marley asked the supervisor to take him to see Herbie as he wanted to see how things were progressing. He, also, wanted to make sure the transport locos were being unloaded. They found Herbie at the loading bay looking rather pleased with himself.

Marley turned to the supervisor. 'You may go now and carry on with your duties.'

'Thank you, Professor, I will leave you to get on with your work, goodbye.'

Marley and Herbie both agreed that the new technology dome was great. Herbie informed Marley that everything was in order, the top-secret project had been successfully placed in the correct part of the dome, and the mini subs had been stored away.

Marley looked at the last transport loco and turned to Herbie. 'Under that sheet is my first ever project.'

'What is it Professor?'

'As soon as it is in the shed, I will show you.'

They continued to check the equipment had been placed in the correct locations. One of the unloading crew informed Marley that his project had been placed in the custom-built steel shed that he had designed. Marley, with Herbie in tow, made his way to the shed. Marley opened the small door which had been built into the large door and they both stepped inside. Marley flicked the switch on the wall and the lights came on.

Marley looked at his first ever project and felt all nostalgic for a moment.

Herbie looked at the project. 'It's an old war of the Prawn's sub, Cat Bowl class, Professor.'

'You know your history and you are correct.'

'Is it original Professor?'

'Well, the shell is original, but the inside is completely different.'

'Oh. I guess it is a museum piece as there are no propeller's Professor?'

'It is completely operational. I fitted a jet propulsion system. It is, also, ultra-quiet for covert operations.'

'Does it have a name Professor?'

'Yes, she is called Brave Paw.'

They both stood for about twenty minutes discussing the sub. Marley explained that the sub now only needed four crew to operate it. The deck had been modified so that two mini subs could dock with the sub.

As Jacob arrived at the new technology dome, he noticed that all the construction equipment had gone. He parked his sports F-4 mini and made his way to the entrance. He entered the dome and immediately began scouring for mistakes as the work was now completed, but did it come up to his high standards.

Jacob scrutinised the entrance looking for mistakes in the workmanship. He didn't find any mistakes. The current supervisor was strolling towards the entrance looking forward to going home. Spotting Jacob, his breathing quickened and beads of sweat formed on his brow. Jacob spotted the supervisor and called out to him to come over. The supervisor marched straight over to Jacob.

Standing in front of Jacob still breathing quickly and with beads of sweat on his brow. 'Hello, Master Lord Jacob.'

'Hello, I see you have finished and on time.'

'Yes, Master Lord Jacob. The dome is ready for your inspection.'

'Very good, and I will be checking that you have completed everything to my specifications.'

'This way Master Lord Jacob, if you please.'

Jacob and the supervisor started the tour of the new technology dome. They ambled towards the kitchen first. Jacob was shown that all the modern appliances had been installed as per his instructions, which included a frost, free fridge to store the milk in. Next, they headed for the living quarters. These were also found to be in perfect order, the green leather sofa and the solid oak floor came up to Jacobs high standards. At this point the supervisor's breathing slowed down and he was no longer sweating. He was also in shock as he was getting praise for his work. They continued the tour of the dome and there were no problems to report so far. They reached the top, secret part of the dome.

Jacob looked at the supervisor his armed folded. 'Open this door now. I want to see inside.'

'But Master Lord Jacob, you must be escorted at all times.'

'Open the door now and don't give me orders.'

The supervisor entered the door code and Jacob entered the room alone. He was gone for five minutes before retuning.

'Thank you, everything is in order and you may now continue with the tour.'

'Thank you, Master Lord Jacob. This way.'

They continued with the tour with a visit to the concept room, and again everything was in order and finished to Jacobs high standards.

'Now, I wish to see the loading bay and it had better come up to standard to match the rest of the dome.'

'It does Master Lord Jacob.'

They set of at a steady stroll towards the loading bay. Approaching the loading bay, Jacob noticed that the doors were larger and the layout had been altered.

Jacob stamped his foot and raised his voice. 'Why has the loading bay not been constructed and completed as per my orders?'

'Well Master Lord Jacob, Prof-'

'I don't want excuses. I want this redoing and to my original plans.' Jacob stamped his foot.

A cat could be heard shouting from outside. 'It's my fault. I redesigned it to my specifications as the loco transport would not fit.'

Marley marched through the loading bay doors.

Jacob froze to the spot for a second. 'Hello Professor Marley. Sorry, I was not informed of your design change.'

'No problem and no harm done, and in here it's just Professor.'

'Yes, Professor but I was not informed of your arrival.'

'I wanted no fuss and I just wanted to oversee the unloading of the equipment.'

Jacob spun round to face his supervisor and placed a paw on his left shoulder. 'Why was I not informed that Professor Marley was here? You have embarrassed me.'

'I did not think that it was important Master Lord Jacob.'

'That is ok and it will not happen again. You're Fired!'

The now old supervisor turned and scurried out of the loading bay doors nearly knocking Herbie over, who was finishing off checking the equipment.

Marley stood and looked at Jacob. *I must improve his people skills.*

Marley walked over to Jacob and patted him on the shoulder, 'You were a bit harsh on the poor lad Major.'

'They need to learn Lieutenant Colonel.'

'Yes, they do. Now it's good to see you.'

'It's good to see you after so long.'

They both agreed that for appearance, sake that Jacob would address Marley as Professor, and Marley would address Jacob as Master Lord Jacob so as not to arouse any suspicion. This was due to the fact that they were both retired members of C.A.T. (Covert Aquatics Team.) and it was a secret. They exited through the loading bay doors to the outside. They could see that all the equipment had been sorted into the relevant piles.

Jacob tapped Marley on the arm. 'Who is that over there?'

'That is my assistant, Herbie, and he is very good at his job. He is also very trust worthy.'

'Does he know about us and C.A.T.?'

'No. He only knows about me and that I had a unit.'

'Well, my top cat, Oliver, knows about me and that I was part of a unit. He is also very trustworthy.'

'I have a surprise in the shed that you might like.'

They ambled towards the steel shed, Jacob wondering what the surprise could be as the shed happened to be rather large. Reaching the shed, Marley opened the smaller door and stepped inside. Marley switched the lights on. Jacob followed closely behind. Once inside, Jacob just stood with his mouth wide open gawping at what he saw.

'Well Jacob, do you like the surprise?'

'Yes. It's Brave Paw, our first sub, that we served on together.'

'I didn't think you would recognize her after all this time.'

'How could I forget the elegant shape of her steel hull.'

'Well wait until you see what I have done to the interior as I have made a few minor alterations.' Marley smiled and patted Jacob on the shoulder. 'Let go and have a bite to eat and a drink, and I'll tell you all about the alterations I have made to Brave Paw.'

As they headed for the kitchen, they passed Herbie, and Marley told him to finish off the last of the boxes then he would be done for the day.

# CHAPTER 6

Jacob and Marley sat at the solid oak table in the kitchen drinking their milk and eating salmon sandwiches, sitting in silence until they had finished. They cleaned up and sat back down at the table to reminisce about their time on Brave Paw during the war of the Prawns.

Marley recalled the time when he was on duty and had to give the orders to go into enemy territory and rescue some stricken sailors from an enemy camp controlled by Thomas Katz and R2. This Marley recalled was the beginning of the Covert Aquatics Team been formed. They also carried out reconnaissance raids and rescue missions during the war.

Jacob recalled some of his memories of the war. His favourite one was the time they had been at sea for a month, and how during the entire time the chef had failed to serve bacon on his breakfast. So, upon returning to port after a successful rescue mission, he had fired the chef, the first of many.

Marley chuckled to himself. 'I am guessing nothing has changed with you firing chefs then.'

'No, I fired my last chef for the same reason, no bacon on my breakfast.'

'You must go through some chefs.'

'One or two.'

'You mean one or two hundred.'

Jacob grinned before he answered. 'Maybe a few hundred, my head cat, Oliver, will know the exact figure for the palace.'

'I will have to ask him some time.'

They continued recalling their war time adventures for the next hour.

Marley stood up. 'Well, do you want to see what I have done to the interior of Brave Paw?'

'Yes. Let's go and see what you have done to Brave Paw.'

Once outside they headed for the shed that housed Brave Paw. As they entered the shed, Marley switched on the lights and there was the sub.

'I thought you said it was fully restored.'

'It is fully restored, except for my alterations, and before you ask, it is fully operational.'

'But there are no propellers.'

'That is because I have installed a jet propulsion system to make her ultra-quiet.' Marley laughed.

'I cannot wait to see the inside.'

They used the tall, steel steps that were next to the sub to climb up onto the deck. They then climbed up the conning tower and entered the sub. Once inside, Marley switched on the lights and the systems used to operate the sub. Jacob looked around at how the bridge he remembered had changed. For one, the diving control panels were now computerized on a large screen listing depth, speed and direction. There was now a chair where the periscope once stood, but there was still a wooden steering wheel for steering the sub.

After Jacob had finished looking around, he looked at Marley. 'Why is there a chair in the middle of the bridge instead of a periscope?'

'The chair is in the middle of the bridge so the captain can see everything that is going on. I removed the periscope to reduce the risk of detection. I have installed a camera that can see what is on the surface at a depth of 50 feet using infra-green light and has a range of 10 leagues.'

'You really have redesigned the bridge and installed new technology. Why have you left the wheel to steer the sub when we have guidance technology that can steer the sub?'

'I trust and like the wheel, plus I wanted to keep something original on the bridge.' Marley grinned.

'It looks much better now and no longer cramped like I remember.'

'All you need is two people to run the bridge now as the captain can control everything from his chair in an emergency, if needed.'

Marley continued explaining how everything else worked on the bridge. The crowning glory was when Marley pressed one of the buttons on the captain's chair and a blind opened like a pair of curtains, this revealed a clear view of the outside world. He explained that nobody could see in as it was a view from eight cameras that had been mounted on the bow to create the view of the outside world, and the live video was shown on the big screen. Marley pressed the button on the captain's chair and the screen was covered by the blinds. He then showed Jacob the rest of the sub and all the changes that had been made. He explained that the galley had been fitted out with all the modern appliances. The only room that was totally original was the torpedo room.

Jacob turned and looked at Marley. 'You have done wonders with the sub.'

'Thank you, but I could not see her rot and then turned into scrap.'

They left the sub and headed back to the kitchen. When they reached the kitchen, Marley poured two glasses of milk and they both sat down. As they sat drinking their milk Jacob asked Marley about the new top-secret sub.

'The new, top-secret sub, a Cat Tree class, is now complete and ready for sea trials.'

'Have you arranged the sea trials as I would like to see how it does.' Jacob rubbed his paws together.

'I have arranged the sea trials and it would be an honour for you to come on the sea trial. The new Cat Tree class sub is now the best submarine in the world as it has all the top technology installed and is ultra-silent. This is due to the hull been covered in my new sonar absorbing paint.' Marley finished his milk. 'I will give you a tour of the new sub.'

Jacob finished his milk and they walked steadily towards the top, secret part of the lab. As they made their way across the dome Herbie came running towards them.

'Professor Marley!'

'Yes, Herbie now calm down.'

'Professor I have a message for you and it's from the yellow printer.'

'Very well Herbie. Excuse me Master Lord Jacob.'

Marley left Jacob and stepped to one side with Herbie. Herbie handed the print out to Marley.

> Lieutenant Colonel Marley
> Need you to form your old team to go up against the new C.A.T. team in a challenge, as I need to know they are ready to carry out a mission.
> General Sooty.
> P.S. Two days from now.

Marley studied the print out for a few seconds. 'Send a reply. Only know the location of one other team member for the moment.'

'Yes, Professor, I will send the reply but who are the other members?'

'Come with me.'

Marley and Herbie walked back to where Jacob was standing.

Marley waved his paw towards Jacob. 'Herbie, I would like to introduce my second-in-command, Major Jacob.'

Jacob and Herbie both shook paws.

Marley put his paw on Jacob's shoulder. 'Are you up for a challenge and showing them new recruits how it's done?'

'Yes sir. What about Hal? We will need a driver as Sweep died two years ago.'

'I don't know where Hal is, but I can get a top driver,' said Marley.

'How long before the challenge, sir?'

'Two days. I will call General Sooty to find out more about this challenge.'

'I will be ready sir.'

'Very good Major.'

Before Jacob left for the palace, he phoned Oliver and told him to get his equipment ready as he was going on a challenge.

Marley and Herbie headed for the top-secret part of the dome so they could be alone when discussing the challenge.

When they were both secure in the top-secret lab, Herbie stood next to Marley. 'Do you want to be alone during the phone call with General Sooty, Professor?'

'No, you can stay. You are trustworthy after all.'

'Thank you, Professor.'

Marley picked up the yellow phone and dialled General Sooty's direct line.

'Hello, this is General Sooty.'

'Hello sir, this is retired Lieutenant Colonel Marley I am calling about the challenge you have set, sir.'

'The challenge that I have set is to see which team can remove a ball from a cone set on the beach. The approach will be from the sea using submarines. You must remain undetected during the entire challenge. Are you up for the challenge Lieutenant Colonel?'

'Yes sir, my team can do this.'

'Very good and my team will use the new Cat Tree class sub.'

'Yes, sir and we will use my Cat Bowl class sub.'

'Very good Lieutenant Colonel see you at the harbour in two days.'

Marley put the phone down. He turned to Herbie and said that he would need his special C.A.T. equipment from storage, and both subs needed to be transported to the harbour ready for the challenge. Herbie said that he would arrange that and get Marley's equipment out of storage. Marley arranged for George to be at the harbour in two days.

# CHAPTER 7

Two days later, Marley, Jacob and George were stood on the quayside. The harbour had been cordoned off to stop anyone seeing the new Cat Tree class sub. They were waiting for the other team to arrive and begin the challenge. It was a warm sunny start to the day with no wind, so the sea was calm.

'A good day for a challenge as the conditions are perfect major,' Marley commented.

'Yes sir. The conditions are perfect.'

While they waited Marley asked George to go aboard the sub and familiarize himself with the controls and the layout before the challenge.

As Marley and Jacob checked their equipment on the quayside, Jacob looked up at Marley. 'Where did you find George?'

'Top Paw, and he is the best they had.'

'So, George is one of the new breeds of military cats who are trained in army and navy tactics sir.'

'He is from the sub core unit programme, and it is a huge success for C.A.T. as they are trained to operate subs and how to do covert missions.'

'But has he seen combat sir?'

'No. He has only had simulated combat missions, but he knows how to handle himself. Just trust me, Jacob.'

'I trust you, sir.'

The other team arrived on the quayside ready for the challenge. A continental 1700 car drove onto the quayside and pulled up near to them. General Sooty stepped out of the car and ambled towards the two groups of cats.

He stood in front of the cats. 'Good morning, and I hope you are all ready for the challenge that I have set.'

'Yes, sir,' both groups echoed.

'Well with that established, you may board your respective boats, while I discuss the details of the challenge with both Lieutenant Colonels.'

As the cats headed for their respective subs, General Sooty turned towards Marley. 'Good to see you again Lieutenant Colonel.'

'Good to see you too sir.'

'I see you found Major Jacob. Who is your driver?'

'We have Captain George from One Paw sir as our driver and I am pleased I found Major Jacob.'

'Right, let's get down to business and the details of the challenge shall we.'

They stood on the quayside and General Sooty explained the rules of the challenge to both cats. They had to remain undetected during the challenge. To make things a little bit harder cameras had been placed on the beach to see if they could complete the whole challenge undetected.

General Sooty faced both cats and saluted. 'Good luck and may the best team win, and I will see you both in two hours at the beach.'

'Yes sir,' both cats echoed together and saluted back.

Both cats headed for their respective subs to get ready for the challenge ahead. Once on board, Marley gathered Jacob and George on the bridge ready to explain the challenge to them.

'Right, Major Jacob and Captain George, our challenge for today is; we have to sail to the beach on the other side of the bay on sector 6. Once we reach the bay, myself and Major Jacob will go ashore and remove a ball from a cone on the beach, while remaining undetected.'

'What am I to do sir?' said George.

'You are to remain on the sub and stay undetected until the challenge is over.'

'Yes, sir.'

'Only one more thing Major, we will have to exit via the hatches and swim ashore to see if we can remain undetected.'

While Jacob and George were both checking the hatches were all secure, Marley sat in the captain's chair and started the warm up checks. They returned to the bridge and reported back to Marley that everything was secure.

Jacob spoke, 'I thought we needed four cats to operate this sub, Lieutenant Colonel?'

'We do Major. Which is why I asked Herbie to join us and help.'

With that Herbie appeared on the bridge 'As soon as we set sail, I will serve ice cold milk and bacon sandwiches Professor.'

'Very good Herbie.'

Herbie returned to the galley to prepare the bacon sandwiches.

Marley got out of the captain's chair. 'Captain George, you can now take control.'

'Yes, Lieutenant Colonel.' George sat in the captain's chair and engaged the jet propulsion system and Brave Paw moved away from the quayside and headed towards the open sea.

Herbie appeared on the bridge. 'The bacon sandwiches will be ready in five minutes and will be served in the wardroom. George, you will have to eat in your chair.' Herbie left the bridge and returned to the galley.

Marley and Jacob departed the bridge and headed for the wardroom. Once inside the wardroom, Herbie served the bacon sandwiches and the milk.

'Thank you, Herbie, now go and serve yourself and George.'

Herbie closed the wardroom door. Marley and Jacob ate their sandwiches and drank their milk. They discussed how they were going to complete the challenge. Both agreed that they would use the inflatable raft to row ashore, and land on the beach where the undergrowth was the densest. They would then make their way to the beach and Jacob would go and remove the ball from the cone. When Jacob had the ball, they would fire a red flare to signal the end of the challenge. They both sat and finished their milk.

Marley and Jacob left the wardroom and marched straight to the bridge.

Arriving on the bridge, Marley walked straight over to George. 'Can I have an update on our progress.'

'We are at a depth of 150 feet, speed 10 knots, a heading of 185 degrees and ten minutes from the drop of point.'

'Very good. You have made excellent progress. It will soon be time to depart the sub.' Marley rubbed his paws together. 'Slow to 3 knots and make your depth of 20 feet.'

George carried out Marley's orders, and Herbie was asked if there were any sonar contacts other than the other sub. Herbie confirmed that there were no other sonar contacts in the area.

Marley looked around the bridge then at Jacob. 'Let's go and get ready Major, it's time to show the kittens how it's done.'

'Yes Sir. We do need to show them who is the best.'

Marley and Jacob left the bridge to go and get ready for the challenge. When they were both ready, they returned to the bridge wearing their survival suits. Marley gave the order for all stop so that they could exit the sub. George carried out the order and the sub came to a stop.

Before they left the bridge, Marley told George not to do anything irrational and to park straight. Once Marley and Jacob were in the escape trunk, Herbie equalised the pressure and then opened the outer hatch. Marley and Jacob exited the sub and swam to the surface with their equipment. When they reached the surface, the inflatable raft was deployed and they climbed inside. Marley took hold of the oars, rowed for the shore and the dense undergrowth. Reaching the dense undergrowth, they waded ashore. They hid the raft in the undergrowth along with their survival suits. They made their way through the undergrowth watching their every step. When they reached the edge of the undergrowth they stopped.

Marley tapped Jacob on the shoulder. 'Right go and do your thing and get the ball. No showing off mind.'

'As if I would show off.' Jacob chuckled.

Jacob left the cover of the undergrowth and started to make his way to the cone and ball ten feet away. Thirty seconds passed and Jacob returned to the undergrowth. Marley fired the flare gun to confirm that they had completed the task. Moments later another flare was seen from the other end of the beach.

General Sooty left his car and marched down to the beach. 'All clear, the challenge is over.'

Marley and Jacob left the cover of the undergrowth and marched down the beach to where General Sooty was waiting. The other team arrived at the same time as Marley and Jacob to await the outcome of the challenge. The results were handed to General Sooty.

General Sooty looked at the results. 'First the new team. You were unsuccessful as you were detected trying to retrieve the ball from the cone. Marley and Jacob, you passed but I want to see if the ball has been removed.'

He marched over to where the cone had been placed. When he reached the site, he saw that the ball and cone had been replaced with another ball and cone. There were two notes.

Both Marley and Jacob looked at each other and Jacob spoke, 'I left a note and I took the ball and cone as a bit of fun Lieutenant Colonel.'

Marley chuckled. 'Who left the other note?' He then turned to Jacob. 'Show off.'

A private handed General Sooty both notes. General Sooty handed the notes to Marley.

Note left by Jacob,

> Sorry about taking the ball and the cone, but we collect them.
>
> Major Jacob.
>
> P.S. Thanks for the challenge.

Second note found on the beach,

> You are good but I am better, and I put the ball and cone back.
>
> Even if it is an ice cream cone and ping pong ball.
>
> Thanks H

Marley chuckled. 'This note is from Captain Hal, but where is he?'

Marley rotated on the spot to ask Jacob if he knew anything about the whereabouts of Hal, but Jacob was nowhere in sight.

'Has anyone seen Major Jacob?' Marley shouted.

'No, sir,' a private shouted.

Jacob had disappeared into the undergrowth and was busy making his way round to the water's edge. Jacob moved stealthily through the dense undergrowth until he could see a cat stood near to the water's edge. Jacob saw a black and white cat wearing a balaclava, so he removed his Sweep Monty commander knife from his belt and moved swiftly towards the cat.

Jacob put his knife to the cat 's throat. 'Hello Captain Hal.'

'Hello Major Jacob. You can take your knife from my throat now.'

'Ok. You were never in any danger, it's still in the sheath as I didn't want to hurt you captain.'

Jacob then marched Hal back to the beach where General Sooty and Lieutenant Colonel Marley were still waiting.

Jacob walked Hal over to them. 'Look who I found in the undergrowth.'

Marley sniggered. 'Hello Captain Hal and very well done Major.'

'Hello sir, good to see you after so long.'

'You are a top thief but you cannot escape from the Major.'

'Yes, I'm a top thief, but the Major is just too good.'

Marley then introduced Hal to General Sooty. They all stood on the beach discussing the challenge and what Hal was doing on the beach. It turned out that Hal was on his way back from a job he had done when he saw the other crew coming ashore. Hal added that anyone could have spotted them. He noticed the cones on the beach and decided to join in but that backfired when Major Jacob found him in the undergrowth.

General Sooty smiled. 'The real reason behind the challenge was to see if the other team were ready for a mission of the upmost importance. Since they failed it will be up to you, Marley and your team if they want to accept the mission.'

'What is the mission General?' Marley stood to attention.

'A team lead by Thomas Katz and R2 have taken over the dairy run by Mr Pickles on milk island.'

Jacob gripped Marley by the shoulder. 'That's my milk cat who supplies me with my gold top sir.'

'Looks like you have your team sir as Mr Pickles is the Major's milk cat.'

'Thank you, Lieutenant Colonel Marley. I will go and let you get ready for your mission. I will send the details to you as soon as I get back to my office.'

'Thank you, sir.'

With that General Sooty headed back to his car and back to his office. Marley suggested that they all go back to the technology dome and await the mission orders. They left the beach and headed back to the sub. When they were back in the harbour, they left for the technology dome.

# CHAPTER 8

Marley, Jacob, Hal, Herbie and George arrived at the technology dome and headed straight for the kitchen and some well, earned food.

Once they were all in the kitchen and seated at the table, Marley stood next to the cupboards. 'Would anyone like some chicken and salmon sandwiches and a glass of ice-cold milk?'

They all answered together, 'Yes please.'

Marley prepared the sandwiches and Jacob volunteered to pour out the glasses of milk.

Marley sat at the table. 'Well, today was a great success and we showed them kittens how it's done.'

Jacob had a big grin on his face. 'Well, we couldn't let them win, and I got Hal.'

'You're just too good Major, but I had fun.' Hal smiled.

Marley cleared his throat. 'Right, I had better explain a few things to Hal and George.'

Hal and George put down their glasses of milk ready to listen. 'During your time at the dome waiting to go on the mission nobody is to be addressed by their rank. This means that I am to be addressed as Professor Marley and Jacob is to be addressed as Master Lord Jacob. George and Hal, you will be addressed by your first names only.'

Hal tapped his glass. 'Why do I have to address Jacob as Master Lord Jacob?'

Marley tapped his paw on the table. 'It is Jacob's title and you will address him by it while you are here. Do I make myself clear?'

'Yes, Professor Marley.'

'Very good.'

'So how did you both come by your new titles since you left C.A.T. but remain on the reserve list?' Hal said after he had taken a drink of milk.

Marley spoke first. 'I become a professor after the Prawn war. I studied at the Top Paw university in Parkhead where I achieved seventeen PhD's.'

Jacob gave a smile. 'When I was asked to regenerate sector C ten years ago, I took charge of a team and was made a master. When I got my job in the palace it came with the title of Lord. So, I decided to keep both titles and be called Master Lord Jacob.'

Marley looked at Hal. 'So, what have you been up too?'

'I hire myself out to steal things that are in secure places.'

'Well at least you are doing something you are good at.'

Everyone laughed at Marley's comment.

George placed his paws on the table. 'I am from One Paw and can fly, drive, and sail anything on the planet.' George omitted that he hated bad parking.

They sat and continued to discuss what they had all been doing since the war.

They all got a glass of fresh milk when Herbie entered the kitchen carrying a large pile of papers.

Herbie placed the papers on the table. 'Here is the information for the mission Professor.'

'Thank you, Herbie.'

'I will go and wait by the printer in case any more information comes through Professor.'

'Very good and thank you.'

Herbie left the kitchen and marched back to the printer room to wait for more information should it come through.

Marley took the pile of paper and placed it in front of himself. He then split the pile into four equal piles and placed one in front of each of them.

Marley then tapped the table. 'Right, I want you to go through the pile of paper in front of you and sort it out into relevant piles, reconnaissance photos, layout of the dairy etc.'

They all nodded, each picking up a pile of papers and organised them into piles ready for deliberation on the mission later.

Several minutes passed and all the papers had been sorted into the relevant piles. These were reconnaissance photos and piles of information regarding the location, layout and the surrounding area of the milk dairy. All the information was placed together in the relevant piles.

Marley decided that they would go through the intelligence in pairs. Jacob and Hal would go through the reconnaissance photos first, and himself and George would go through the rest. After doing this they could then decide on a plan to take back the dairy. They all got themselves a glass of milk and began to analyse what they had been given. After half an hour had passed, they swapped over their documents with each other and continued to look at the rest of the information.

After another half an hour had passed and they had gone over all the documents, Marley stood up and walked over to the fridge and removed the milk. He poured each of them a glass.

Marley replaced the milk back in the fridge and sat down. 'So, Jacob and Hal have you come up with a plan to retake the dairy?'

Jacob and Hal sat in silence looking at each other for a moment deciding who would go first.

Jacob broke the silence. 'Well, I will go first and put my idea forward for consideration.'

The others sat and looked at Jacob waiting for his idea on how he would retake the dairy.

'I think the best way into the dairy is from the west. First, we land on the beach then go through the forest. This would leave us with the river to cross. We cross the river and its straight up and over the hill and into the dairy from the west side.

Marley made a note of Jacobs plan. 'Right Hal, let's have your idea.

'My plan is almost identical to Jacob's. Except that I would cross the river further downstream. This would eliminate the need to climb the hill. I would then circle round the dairy and enter from the north side as the terrain is less exposed.'

Marley again made a note of the plan. 'Now for my idea. I would land on the east side of the beach. Then I would climb the cliff face then into the forest. Then I would make my way to the dairy and enter from the east side. Right George. Let's have your idea.'

'I would land on the southern beach and go through the forest and head towards the dirt track. Then I would head round to the east and then the rest of the plan is identical to Marley's.'

Marley again made notes.

They discussed how they were going to retake the dairy from Thomas Katz and R2. The reconnaissance photos had shown that there were only six cats guarding the perimeter of the dairy, but not all at once. The photos showed that two of the cats were inside. So, they knew that they would have to take out four cats to gain access to the dairy.

Marley placed a paw on the table. 'We will try and disable the guards first rather than kill them. Once the guards have been disabled, then we will be able to gain access to the dairy with Hal's help as some of the doors are coded.'

'That wouldn't be a problem as long you can cover me when I work my magic.' Hal tapped his paw on the table.'

This made Jacob smile. 'I'll be able to use my B.D.S. as it needs a good workout.'

George scratched his head. 'What's a B.D.S.?'

Marley placed his paws behind his head. 'It's a big, door shotgun that will blow any door clean off its hinges. It is also very loud so everyone will know that we are there.'

George rubbed his paws together. 'I might have to give that a try one day. So, what are we to do with Thomas Katz and R2 if we capture them?'

Marley turned his head and stared straight at Jacob. 'They are to be taken alive but they must not to escape and go free. Do you understand?'

'Yes sir, they are not to escape.' Jacob shrugged his shoulders.

'Yes, but the army want them taken alive for questioning.'

'That'll spoil all my fun. As you wish sir.'

'Very good Jacob, but I'm sure you will still have some fun. Now let's all have a break and a glass of milk before continuing to decide the final plan of attack.'

Marley rose from his chair and ambled over to the fridge and removed a bottle of milk and poured everyone a glass. With the milk back in the fridge, they sat and drank their milk in silence. Marley finished his milk and placed his glass on the table. Picking up the notes, he studied them, analysing what each one had suggested for the plan of attack. He had all the reconnaissance photos laid out on the table and he was studying them. He was aware that two of them wanted to access the dairy from the east side, one from the west and one from the north.

Marley marked the map to show the plan of attack that each of them had given, standing with his paws on the table studying all of the routes that they had given for the mission.

Herbie entered the room, and marched straight over to Marley. 'Would you all like some food Professor?'

'Yes, that would be great, it might help as we are having a problem trying to find the best route into the dairy.'

Herbie reached over and grabbed the map with all the routes marked on, tapping his paw on the table he looked up. 'Professor, why don't you land on the south beach and go straight up and through the main gates?'

They all stood up and looked at the map and began to study what Herbie had just suggested. After a few minutes they all looked at each other and nodded.

Marley turned to Herbie and placed a paw on his shoulder. 'You are a genius. That is the direct route. Why not?'

'I just thought why not go and knock on the front door and Professor you are the genius.'

'We will have to make you an honorary C.A.T. captain and yes we are ready for some food.'

Jacob interrupted. 'We will all go to my palace and have some food. I will just let my top cat, Oliver, know that we will be having tea at the palace.'

Herbie took Jacob into the office so he could ring Oliver and make the arrangements. They all headed back to the palace. Once they were at the palace, Marley, Herbie, Hal and George could not believe that the staff were scurrying around the palace in a blur when Jacob entered.

Oliver approached Jacob at a slow marching pace. 'Everything is in order Master Lord Jacob.'

'Very good Oliver. You have done well.'

Jacob introduced everyone to Oliver.

Oliver escorted them to the main formal dining room. As they were seated at the solid oak table, Herbie stood in the doorway.

Jacob raised his head and looked at Herbie. 'What are you doing?'

'I am only Professor Marley's assistant Master Lord Jacob so I will go and eat with the staff.'

'You are my guest so you will eat with us.'

Oliver seated Herbie at the table. They had a meal of chicken soup for starters. A main meal of salmon and prawn salad and rice pudding for dessert.

After they had finished their meal, Jacob loaded his equipment into the troop carrier and they all headed back to the new technology dome to prepare for the mission.

# CHAPTER 9

Arriving back at the technology dome, Jacob parked in the loading bay. They all climbed out of the troop carrier.

Marley closed the passenger door. 'Can you make sure all of the equipment for the mission is loaded into the troop carrier please Herbie.'

'I will see to it professor.'

'Thankyou.'

Herbie left and made his way inside to make sure that the equipment had been placed in order ready to be loaded into the troop carrier. Marley in the meantime had gone to the workroom and telephoned the people at One Paw to arrange for the four kittens from the challenge to be at the harbour in the morning at 05.00 hours. He also made arrangements for both mini subs to be taken to the harbour and attached to Brave Paw.

Marley left the workroom and found Jacob still at the loading bay. 'Come with me I have a surprise for you.'

Jacob and Marley ambled to the top-secret part of the laboratory. Once they were both inside of the room, Marley closed the door. He walked over to a wooden glass fronted cabinet and opened it. He removed a small weapon and handed it to Jacob.

Jacob took the weapon from Marley. 'What is this sir.'

'It is a new type of laser gun that I have developed.'

'How will this be of any use on the mission?'

'Well, it has a range of ten yards and it fires a laser beam that will blow any door of its hinges, quietly.' Marley patted Jacob on the back.

'But I have my B.D.S. and it needs a workout.'

'You can use that as back up.'

'Thank you, sir.'

They left the top-secret room and went to find Hal and George. They located them in the kitchen, and made sure that they were ready for the mission. They left the kitchen and made their way to the loading bay.

Marley walked over to the troop carrier. 'Herbie has everything been loaded correctly for the mission.'

Herbie looked at his clip board and ran his paws over the check list. 'Everything is present and correct Professor.'

'Thank you, Herbie, you are a great help.'

Marley shouted, 'Everyone into the troop carrier.'

They all marched straight over and climbed into the troop carrier. With George at the wheel, they headed for the harbour. Arriving at the harbour, George parked next to Brave Paw. They climbed out of the troop carrier and began to unload the equipment onto the quayside. Marley looked up and noticed both mini subs had been attached to the deck of Brave Paw.

Jacob placed the last bag on the quayside. 'George, Hal take your equipment on to the sub.'

The crew from the challenge were marching along the quayside towards Marley.

Marley noticed that Jacob had all of his equipment on the quayside. 'Are you ready to board Major?'

'Yes, sir'

'I will be along in a moment Major.'

Jacob picked up his equipment and boarded the sub.

Marley stood on the quayside with the crew from the challenge. 'Right, I expect you kittens to perform exceptionally well on this mission as the fate of the Gold Top depends upon it.'

The captain saluted Marley. 'My team will not let you down sir.'

Marley picked up his equipment from the quayside. 'Captain, you and your team are to board the sub at once.' Marley boarded the sub.

Marley placed his equipment with the rest and noticed Jacob checking his equipment. 'Is everything in order Major?'

Jacob stopped checking the equipment and stood up to face Marley. 'Everything is in order sir and all the equipment had been stored correctly.'

'Very good Major.' Marley then made his way to the bridge. 'Captain everything is in order and we are ready to set sail.'

The captain turned to his team. 'I want all checks completing to make sure that we are were ready to set sail.'

The crew left the bridge and preceded around the sub doing their checks. With the checks completed they reported back to the captain that everything had been secured and they were ready to set sail.

The captain stood on the bridge and gave the order to set sail. The jet propulsion system was engaged and Brave Paw eased away from the quayside and headed for the open sea.

They cleared the harbour and were out in the open sea, the captain sat in his chair. 'Submerge the boat to a depth of 100 feet and set a course for Milk Island.'

Marley looked around the bridge as the crew carried out the orders. 'Captain, myself and my team will be in the wardroom going over the mission details if you need us. Stop one mile from the shore and inform me of any contacts along the route.'

'Yes, Lieutenant Colonel.'

Marley left the bridge and strolled to the wardroom. He opened the wardroom door and stepped inside. The others were already seated around the table ready to begin discussing the mission details. Marley poured himself a glass of milk and sat down. They started to go over the mission details. They had been going over the mission for just over an hour when there was a knock at the door.

George, who was closest to the door, stood up and opened it. 'What do you want midship?'

'I want to know if you want some chicken sandwiches and some more milk captain?'

George asked the others and they all said yes, the midship closed the door and went to get the sandwiches and milk. The midship returned a few moments later and left the sandwiches and milk on the table.

About hour later there was another knock at the door. This time Marley got up from his chair and walked over to the door and opened it.

'Hello midship'. What do you want?'

'We are one mile from the shore Lieutenant Colonel Marley.'

'Thank you midship'. We will make sure everything is in order ready for our departure.'

'I will inform the captain Lieutenant Colonel Marley.'

The midshipman left and went to inform the captain that they were just performing the last-minute checks ready for departure.

Marley checked his equipment over making sure that it was in order. 'Can you all load your equipment into the mini subs.' Marley rubbed his paws together. 'Jacob and Hal, you will be using the mini sub to the right of the conning tower as myself and George are using the one to the left.'

Once the equipment had been loaded onto the respective mini subs, they headed for the bridge.

Arriving on the bridge, Marley made his way over to the captain. 'Get half a mile from the shore for our departure, then go out to sea two miles and wait for our signal.'

'Yes, Lieutenant Colonel.'

Marley and his team left the bridge and headed for their respective mini subs.

Just as they left the bridge, George turned his head. 'Captain, make sure you park straight.'

Reaching their respective mini subs, they climbed aboard. The start-up checks were completed and the captain was informed that they were ready for departure. Both mini subs lifted off from the deck of Brave Paw and soon disappeared into the darkness heading towards the shore. After five minutes, they reached the shore and climbed out of the mini subs securing them on the shore using the undergrowth as cover. The equipment was unloaded from the mini subs and they headed deeper into the undergrowth. They came across a small clearing covered by trees. They removed their water suits and put on their combat suits. Jacob placed his B.D.S gun over his shoulder and placed his laser gun next to his Sweep Monty combat knife on his belt. Marley placed his laser gun next to his Sweep Monty combat knife on his belt. George picked up his feral gun and armed it ready for use. They all turned and looked at Hal who was busy putting a squeaky hammer, a plastic ball on string, a stethoscope and a coat hanger into a bag.

Hal looked up and noticed that they were all staring at him. 'What, you know I don't use technology.'

Marley chuckled. 'Nothing ever changes with you. Let's move out and go and save the Major's milk cat.'

They ambled along through the undergrowth checking for booby traps. They encountered no problems making their way through the dense undergrowth. When they reached the edge of the undergrowth, they could see the road that led up to the main gates of the dairy.

Jacob stopped at the edge of the undergrowth. 'Strange, no blockades and its eerily quiet.'

Marley surveyed the immediate area then turned to Jacob and George. 'You two go ahead and do a reconnaissance of the area and report back here with your findings. Myself and Hal will wait by the road and monitor the immediate area for any activity.'

Jacob and George disappeared into the undergrowth and started to make their way towards the main gates. They were ambling along checking for booby traps as they proceeded.

They were getting close to the main gates when Jacob tapped George on the shoulder, 'Get down I hear a vehicle coming along the road.'

They both looked at the road and waited to see what was coming. A milk tanker appeared so they followed the milk tanker along the road using the undergrowth as cover. When they reached the main gates, they noticed that there were two guards at the gate. The guards opened the gates after checking the driver and truck over. The milk tanker entered the dairy and the guards closed the main gates, remaining outside of the gates. Jacob and George returned to Marley and Hal to report their findings.

Jacob removed his hat and sighed. 'We have a small problem there are two guards on the main gate.'

Marley stood up. 'I thought it was odd that no blockades had been placed on the road.'

'I will take care of them and open the gates at the same time.' Jacob smiled as he started to remove his B.D.S gun from his shoulder.

Marley placed a paw on his head. 'No, they will hear you. How did they open the gates?'

'They took a padlock off to open them.'

'I have an idea. We will use my secret weapon.'

Jacob, Hal and George all spoke at once, 'What secret weapon?'

'Just wait and see.' Marley chuckled. 'Jacob, Hal go and find out where the other four guards are in the dairy. Myself and George will wait near the main gates and observe.'

Jacob and Hal soon disappeared out of sight into the undergrowth, split up and continued to make their way around the perimeter of the dairy looking for the four guards.

# CHAPTER 10

Jacob and Hal returned to Marley and George at the main dairy gates.

Jacob removed his hat and wiped his brow with his paw. 'There are two guards in the bottling plant and two guards at the loading bay. The two guards at the loading bay are busy loading the milk tanker. The milk tanker is round the back of the dairy, the driver is busy helping with his collection and he seems to be unarmed.'

Marley rubbed his chin. 'Well done Major. What did you find during your reconnaissance captain?'

Hal rubbed his paws together. 'The other two guards are in the bottling plant holding the workers at gun point. Both guards are armed with c-3 pistols. The workers are in a small room located next to the bottling plant.'

'Well done captain. What about Thomas Katz and R2?'

Jacob patted Hal on the back. 'Thomas Katz and R2 are in the main office that is located above the loading bay. We were unable to locate Mr Pickles during our reconnaissance of the dairy.'

Marley rubbed his chin again. 'We will deal with the guards and Thomas Katz and R2 first then find Mr Pickles.'

They sat in the undergrowth looking at the main gate waiting to see if the guards would leave. Half an hour passed and the guards were still at their post.

Jacob pointed towards the main gate. 'It's time we made a move, we have to save the dairy and my milk cat.'

George and Hal nodded in agreement with Jacob, it was time to retake the dairy.

Jacob started to reach for his B.D.S gun when Marley gripped his arm. 'It is time for my secret weapon.'

'What secret weapon?' Jacob, George and Hal echoed together.

Marley gave a big grin. 'Hal, get ready to go and remove the padlock from the gates.'

Hal picked up his bag and placed it on his back ready to go when ordered.

Marley took George to one side away from Jacob and Hal. 'Do you see them two guards Captain?'

'Yes, what about them?'

'Well, that shuttle is what they parked across two bays and not even straight.'

'That is bad parking.'

'Well, you go and tell them.' Marley smiled

'I will.' George grinned and rubbed his paws together.

They returned to Jacob and Hal.

Marley crouched down next to Jacob. 'George, you and Hal go and open the main gates and do it quietly.'

Hal turned to face Marley. 'It's me Lieutenant Colonel.'

They made their way down to the road side through the undergrowth.

Reaching the edge of the road they stopped.

Hal crouched down. 'I will wait until the coast is clear before coming to open the gates.'

George left the cover of the undergrowth and stepped onto the road. 'I won't be long.'

George marched along the road towards the main gates. As he approached the main gates the cats got their weapons ready.

One of the cats pointed his weapon at George shouting. 'Where are you going?'

George thought for a second before speaking. 'I am here to collect the shuttle.'

'I was not told about this.' The cat held his weapon and kept it pointed at George.

'You can ask Thomas Katz or R2 if you wish to disturb them.'

'The keys are in the ignition.' The cat pointed to the shuttle.

'Thank you. One more thing who parked this shuttle?'

'I did why?' One of the cats said.

The next thing that Marley, Jacob and Hal saw were the two guards laid on the road knocked out by George. Hal left the cover of the undergrowth and ran towards the gates ready to remove the padlock. He passed George who was stood over the two guards and heard him say, 'I hate bad parking.' Hal continued running to the gates.

Meanwhile in the undergrowth, Jacob glanced at Marley. 'I like your secret weapon, but what was it all about?'

'Oh, he hates bad parking.' Marley chuckled.

Hal reached the gates and placed his bag of tools on the ground. By the time Marley and Jacob arrived, Hal was putting his piece of wire away and the padlock had been removed. George in the meantime had finished tying up the two guards and placed them to the right of the main gates.

With all of them together at the gates, Marley tapped on the gate. 'Jacob, you and George go to the loading bay, myself and Hal will free the workers from the bottling plant.'

Marley and Hal entered the dairy through the main gates and saw various buildings made from stone and wood. They started to make their way to the bottling plant using wooden grates, empty bottles and milk churns as cover. Reaching the washroom, they stopped and leaned against the stone wall. The only way to the bottling plant was to go round the back otherwise they would be seen. This would make freeing the workers a bit more awkward. Marley and Hal shuffled along the side of the washroom and stopped at the end of the building.

They stood motionless for a moment contemplating how they were going to free the workers from the two guards.

Marley reached towards his belt. 'I have my laser gun.'

'I have a pineapple in my bag.'

'Right. You throw the pineapple through the window of the bottling plant then in we go.'

Hal removed the pineapple from his bag and pulled the pin. Scurrying over the cobbled yard he pasted the window and threw the pineapple into the room. There was a loud bang and a flash of bright, white light in the room for a second.

Marley had moved from the corner of the building, over the cobbled yard and was now positioned at the door. After the pineapple exploded, he kicked the wooden door open. The guard went for his gun but Marley shot him in the leg disabling him.

The second guard already had his gun at the ready and it was pointed straight at Marley. Before the guard had time to pull the trigger Hal hit him with his squeaky hammer on the back of his head knocking him unconscious.

They tied the two guards up and located the workers in a small room next to the bottling plant.

Hal untied them and Marley stood in the doorway. 'Wait here until the area is secure.'

They left the workers and headed to the loading bay to meet up with Jacob and George.

Jacob and George entered the dairy through the main gates and started to head towards the loading bay. The best route they had decided earlier was to go past the stores building and then onto the loading bay. Reaching the store building, they stopped leaned against the stone wall for a moment to assess the situation. They could see the loading bay from where they were stood.

Jacob was looking around the loading bay from the corner of the stores building and he turned to George. 'Looks like it's just them two guards. No sign of the driver that I can see.'

'I can only see the two guards as well. That driver might be a problem though.'

'Yes, but we don't have time to wait and find out, we need to get going.'

They stood for a moment and finally decided that they would go down the side of the stores building to get to the loading bay. When they reached the end of the stores building, they would take out the two guards and hope the driver did not try to be a hero.

Creeping along the side of the stores building they reached the end, ran over the cobbles and headed straight for the loading bay. George was the first to shoot and he shot one of the guards in the left arm. The guard reacted by reaching for his gun with his right hand so George shot him dead.

Jacob meanwhile crept up behind the other guard, taking his commando knife he placed it on the guard's throat. 'Don't move or you will join your mate.'

The guard nodded to agree with Jacob because moments earlier his colleague had been shot dead.

Jacob had his back to the truck and the driver. The truck driver who had heard the shooting had made his way round the truck and he was now positioned behind Jacob. He took his gun and aimed it at Jacob.

Marley and Hal came running round the corner of the loading bay.

Marley saw the driver had his gun pointed at Jacob and shouted, 'George bad parking.'

George swivelled on the spot aimed his gun at the driver and shot him in the leg. The driver fell to the ground and gave himself up.

The driver and the remaining guard were both tied up and placed in the corner of the loading bay.

Since George had killed a guard, Marley reminded them that Thomas Katz and R2 were to be taken alive if possible. They were to capture both and wait for the army to arrive to take them and the guards away.

Marley tapped his foot lightly on the floor. 'Hal, work your magic and open the loading bay doors.'

Hal took his squeaky hammer and a screwdriver from his bag. A minute later and the loading bay doors were open.

Marley, Jacob and George had their guns at the ready. They could see that the corridor was clear, so they entered the main building and began to sweep all the downstairs rooms. The downstairs rooms were found to be clear. This meant that Thomas Katz and R2 were upstairs. Jacob headed straight for stone stairs, climbing them first, with his B.D.S. at the ready.

Marley, Hal and George followed closely behind, each one hoping that they did not shoot as Jacob was eager to use his gun. They reached the top of the stairs with no problems. The door on the landing was closed.

Marley moved to one side. 'Hal, work your magic again.'

Jacob started up his B.D.S. gun and fired, there was a loud bang and a lot of smoke. When the smoke cleared, they could see that the door had been completely blown off its hinges, and what was left of it landed flat on the floor.

There was no sign of anybody in the room. There was another door and voices could be heard coming from the other side of it. Marley made a hand signal for Hal to open the door while they stood with their weapons at the ready covering the door.

Hal strolled towards the door when the door suddenly opened and shots were fired. Hal got shot in the right arm. George grabbed Hal and dragged him out of the line of fire.

'Thanks George. I'm ok now go and get them.'

George joined Marley and Jacob and they investigated the room through the open door. They could see Thomas Katz and R2 had retreated into another room and were behind a steel desk, and they both had their guns drawn ready to shoot. Marley took his laser gun and fired a warning shot into the room and blew the milk bottle clock of the wall.

This made Thomas Katz and R2 angry. They started to fire randomly into the room trying to hit one of them. After a few seconds they stopped.

Marley stood behind the door. 'Anyone hurt?'

'No sir.' they all said.

Thomas Katz and R2 kept firing repeatedly every thirty seconds. This meant that Marley, Jacob and George were pinned down. Suddenly there was a loud bang a white flash of light, Hal had thrown a pineapple into the room.

When the light had gone, Thomas Katz and R2 both came running out of the room randomly shooting. R2 only just missed Marley when George shot him in the right leg sending him clattering to the floor. Thomas Katz was still randomly shooting. This annoyed Jacob as he just wanted to shoot him dead, but orders were orders. Jacob took his combat knife from his belt and threw it at Thomas Katz and hit him in the left arm, this only shocked him for a couple of seconds.

George was observing the fight taking place between Jacob and Thomas Katz. He raised his feral gun and shot Thomas Katz in the right leg sending him crashing to the floor.

Marley shouted, 'Well done George.'

'Thankyou sir, anyway he allowed that truck driver to park badly.'

'Secure the prisoners and let's find Jacob's milk cat.'

Jacob and Marley stepped into the other room which looked like an office even with bullet holes in the wall and broken furniture strewn all over the floor. There was no sign of Mr Pickles anywhere in the room. They stood still for a second when Marley heard a noise coming from the cupboard in the corner.

Marley walked over to the cupboard opened the door, there was Mr Pickles. Marley untied him and helped him out of the cupboard.

Mr Pickles stood looking at what was left of his office. 'Thank you for saving my dairy.'

Jacob chuckled. 'It was no trouble at all, you are my milk cat after all and your gold top is the best.'

They patched Hal's arm up and with Mr Pickles all safe they headed back to the bottling plant and told the workers that it was all over. George was left to secure

Thomas Katz and R2 until the army arrived. The five remaining guards and the driver had been placed inside the main gates to the dairy. The workers were tasked with watching over them until the army arrived.

Marley shook Mr Pickles paw. 'The army will not be long so myself and Jacob must go now.'

'Thank you again for saving my dairy and goodbye.'

Marley and Jacob marched out of the main gates, down the road, disappearing into the undergrowth. They made their way back to the beach and the undergrowth. Using the mini subs, they headed back to Brave Paw. Once docked with the sub and they were on board, Marley told the captain to take them home.

# CHAPTER 11

Marley and Jacob sat at the table in the wardroom chatting about how well the mission had gone.

Jacob placed a paw on the table. 'What will happen to Hal and George now that the mission is over?'

'I think Hal will go back to his life of stealing things for others. George is going back to Top Paw and he will be joining C.A.T. at some point.'

They were interrupted by a knock on the door.

Marley shouted, 'Enter.'

A midshipman opened the door and stepped inside. 'Would you both like some breakfast and a glass of milk Lieutenant Colonel Marley?'

'Yes, we will both have a breakfast and a glass of milk thank you, midship'.'

The midshipman spun round and left the wardroom closing the door behind him.

As the door closed Marley turned back to face Jacob, 'Now don't be too hard on them if they get the breakfast wrong.'

'I will try.'

'Good.'

A few minutes passed and the crew member returned to the wardroom with two breakfasts and two glasses of milk and placed them on the table before Marley and Jacob.

Marley looked at the breakfast on the plate and noticed that there was no bacon. *This will not go well with Jacob.*

Jacob noticed that there was no bacon on the plate. 'I want to see the chef now midship'.'

'Yes, Major straight away.'

The midshipman scurried out of the wardroom and thirty seconds later he returned to the wardroom with the chef.

Jacob pointed to his plate then looked straight at the chef. 'Where is my bacon?'

'Sorry Major I forgot to put on the plates.'

'Well, you know what this means don't you?'

'Yes, Major I'm fired.'

Jacob looked at Marley then at the chef. 'No, you are not fired. Just go and get the bacon and hurry.'

The chef was in shock but managed to hold his nerve. 'Yes, Major straight away and thank you.'

The chef and the midshipman both scurried from the room and headed straight for the galley.

Marley tapped gently on the table. 'Well done, you see it is possible.'

'Now don't you get any ideas about me going soft.'

They both chuckled. A few seconds later the chef entered the room with the missing bacon. The chef left and they both tucked into their breakfast. When they had finished breakfast, they headed for the bridge to see the captain.

Marley stood on the bridge. 'Captain, how are we progressing?'

'We should be in port in about ten minutes Lieutenant Colonel Marley.'

'Thank you captain we will be in the wardroom awaiting our arrival in port.'

Fifteen minutes later they had docked in the port. Marley and Jacob collected their equipment and disembarked from the sub. On the quayside they were greeted by General Sooty and Herbie.

General Sooty saluted Marley and Jacob. 'Well done to you both on a successful mission.'

Marley saluted back, 'Thank you, sir.'

'As you both know, officially you were never there.'

'Jacob saluted Sooty. 'Well sir, we are used to it.'

'Well anyway thank you again for saving the dairy and the gold top. Here are two medals, one each.' Sooty placed them in Marley's paw, saluted and left.

Marley took a medal and gave it to Jacob.

Jacob looked at the medal. 'Another one for the collection.'

Marley put his medal in his coat pocket. 'Hello Herbie.'

'Hello Professor. Let's get you both back to the technology dome. I have phoned Oliver who will meet us at the technology dome to take you home Master Lord Jacob.'

'Thank you, Herbie.'

They climbed into Marley's series 2 sports defender and Herbie drove off the quayside and back along the roads to the technology dome. When they reached the technology dome they climbed out of the car and collected their equipment.

As they walked towards the entrance, Herbie stopped. 'Would you both like something to eat and drink.'

They both agreed that it was a good idea, so they all went to the kitchen. As they entered the kitchen Oliver greeted them.

'Hello Master Lord Jacob it's good to see you.'

'It is good to see you too Oliver.'

Oliver placed the ready-made sandwiches on the table with a cold glass of milk.

They sat at the table and tucked into the chicken sandwiches and a glass of milk. With the snack finished, they cleaned up and sat round the table discussing their daily lives.

Jacob tapped his empty glass. 'Well, I think it is about time you had a chef Professor Marley.'

'That's a great idea at least I will get my favourite Saturday breakfast, a bacon and egg sandwich.' Marley sat in his chair and rubbed his paws together and licked his lips.

Herbie was tasked with finding Marley a chef.

Jacob and Oliver then left for the palace with an invitation to return once Marley had a chef. They climbed into the sports f-4 mini and Oliver drove off in the direction of the palace. They chatted during the journey back to the palace. During the journey, Oliver told Jacob that he had made a few changes. The gardener had to keep the driveway clean and the door cat was now responsible for sorting the post.

Arriving back at the palace, Oliver pulled onto the drive and parked at the front of the palace. Jacob noticed that the driveway was clean and tidy. As they entered the palace, Jacob noticed that the staff were busy doing their tasks.

Jacob stood rooted to the spot for a moment. 'I am going to the kitchen and there will be an inspection in ten minutes.'

Jacob opened the kitchen door and stepped in. 'Hello Meg. What is that divine smell?'

'It's only chicken lasagne and rice pudding Master Lord Jacob.'

Jacob had a look on his face like the cat that got the cream. 'My favourite dessert, rice pudding.'

Jacob headed for the exit to go and do the inspection when Meg closed the oven door. 'Tea will be served in half an hour sir.'

'Ok.'

Jacob found Oliver in the lobby waiting to start the inspection. As the inspection started Oliver felt quietly confident that all would go well. They made their way through the palace inspecting every room and the staff as they went. Once the inspection was completed, they both went to Jacob's office.

They sat down after Jacob had poured out two glasses of Gold Top Milk. 'Well, I have trained you well as you seem to be performing miracles. I am very pleased with the progress you have made so far, however, before you get too big for your paws, I must point out a few faults. The garage floor needs cleaning along with the vehicles, the maid has not cleaned the stairs and the door cat had not sorted the post correctly.'

Oliver picked up a pen from the coffee table and made a note of the faults that needed rectifying. 'I guess I will be a lord soon.'

Jacob finished his milk and placed the glass on the coffee table. 'Well, I'm off for tea and no I'm not making you a lord yet.'

'How the other half live. I've got the staff to sort out.'

'Well, you are the manager so bye.' Jacob left the office and headed for the dining room.

After Jacob had eaten his chicken lasagne and rice pudding, he asked for the driver to be sent to his office. There was a knock on Jacob's office door.

'Enter'

The driver entered the office. 'You wanted to see me Master Lord Jacob.'

'Yes, take a seat.'

The driver sat down nervously awaiting his fate.

Jacob sitting behind the desk placed both paws on the desk top. 'Well. I noticed that the garage floor needs cleaning along with all the vehicles. I trust you will see that this happens.'

The driver breathed, a sigh of relief. 'Yes, Sir I will.'

'Well go and get on with the task and next time I may not be as understanding.'

The driver stood up, 'Thank you Master Lord Jacob. I will go and do the tasks immediately.'

As the driver left the office, Oliver entered. 'Hello, you have been summed by Marley as he has a chef.'

Jacob looked up, 'When are we going?'

'In the morning for breakfast at 08.00, but at least Herbie won't need a calendar.' Oliver smiled.

'Funny, ha-ha. I might need one for a new manager.'

Oliver chuckled. 'I have a spare one you can have. I will inform Marley that we will be attending breakfast in the morning.'

Oliver left the office and went to make the arrangements.

The following morning, Jacob and Oliver arrived at the technology dome and were greeted by Herbie who showed them to the dining room where Marley was waiting.

'Morning to you both.'

They both said morning to Marley.

They sat down at the table and Marley poured four glasses of milk.

Marley looked at Jacob. 'Well, I hope the chef is up to your high standards?'

'Well, if not, Oliver has a calendar for Herbie to make a count of the chefs you fire.'

'I will not be needing a calendar thank you.'

'Sorry boss I will do my 200 lines later.'

The chef entered the dining room pushing a trolley with four plates of breakfast on it. The chef took the plates and placed one before each of them.

There was silence as Marley looked at his plate then at the chef. 'Well, what do you think this is?'

'It's your Saturday breakfast Professor.'

'Well correct me if I am wrong, but where is the bacon?'

Oliver and Herbie both glanced in the direction of Jacob waiting for the inevitable.

'Oh, Sorry Prof-.'

Marley banged the table with his paws and looked straight at the chef.

'You're Fired.

**The End'**

## About the author.

Mark lives in the north east of England. A former supermarket worker. He is now a HGV driver and decided to have a go and write a book based on his cat's.

If you enjoyed this book, please add a review on Amazon. Thank you.

Printed in Great Britain
by Amazon